I AM A

Gareth Roberts has written eight previous Doctor Who novels, including *Only Human*, featuring the ninth Doctor, Rose and Captain Jack, together with TV scripts for *Emmerdale*, *Brookside*, *Randall & Hopkirk (Deceased)*, *Swiss Toni* and *Swinging*. He also wrote the Doctor Who interactive adventure *Attack of the Graske* and the mobile phone *Tardisodes* accompanying the 2006 series.

I Am a Dalek

Gareth Roberts

Published by BBC Books, BBC Worldwide Ltd,
Woodlands, 80 Wood Lane, London W12 0TT

First published 2006

ISBN 0 563 48648 1

Commissioning Editor: Stuart Cooper
Consultant Editor: Helen Raynor
Editor: Justin Richards

Doctor Who is a BBC Wales production for BBC ONE
Executive Producers: Russell T Davies and Julie Gardner
Producer: Phil Collinson

Cover design by Henry Steadman © BBC 2006
Typeset in Stone Serif by SX Composing DTP, Rayleigh, Essex
Printed and bound in Great Britain by Bookmarque, Surrey

For more information about this and other BBC books,
please visit our website at www.bbcshop.com

For Terrance Dicks, who got me reading, and
Peter Darvill-Evans, who got me writing

CHAPTER ONE

ROSE CHECKED THE SEAL on her space helmet, then she looked across the TARDIS controls to the Doctor.

'Turning off the air,' he said, his white-gloved hand flicking one of the many switches on the panel. His voice reached Rose through a two-way radio link built into their helmets. 'Turning off the gravity.' He flicked another switch and smiled over at her. Then he remembered something. 'Oh – and balance pressure,' he added, flipping another control. 'Because we don't wanna burst. Going up, Mary Poppins.'

Rose felt the weight leave her body and reached out to steady herself on the edge of her side of the panel. 'Can't believe it,' she said. She cast a glance to the police box doors, imagining what lay outside. 'Walking on the moon.'

'More like leaping,' said the Doctor happily. To demonstrate, he put one foot forward and let himself be carried through the vacuum, landing with the grace of a ballet dancer a good fifteen feet away. 'Practise, then,' he told Rose. 'You don't want to fall flat on your backside out there. Leap!'

Rose let go of the panel and followed his example, remembering to push gently, and landing only a little less expertly right next to him.

'Giant leap. And leap!' the Doctor encouraged her, and they set off, floating and bumping around the TARDIS together.

Rose grabbed one of the wall struts, kicked off and made a perfect cartwheel, watching the large room circle around her.

The Doctor beamed at her. 'Got it? Good.' He reached for a long white pole and a battered old bag that he'd tied to one of the floor plates before turning off the gravity. From the bag he produced a long line of string with flags of all the nations strung along it. 'The bit we've landed on won't be explored for a few thousand years, so let's give 'em a shock when they get there.' He looked along the line, considering, and halted at a green and blue flag with a thick black and yellow stripe along the middle. 'Tanzania?' he said mischievously. Then his eyes lit on the next flag along, which featured a crest and the initials WI. 'No, gotta be this! Women's Institute.' His face fell just for a second. 'We can't.' Then he smiled again and attached the flag to the pole. 'We can! And did those feet, in ancient times, walk upon the moon's mountains green? That'll keep a few historians in jobs in the forty-ninth century.'

The abandoned string of flags hung in the air before Rose's face. Suddenly the importance of what was about to happen struck her. 'Wait a sec,' she told the Doctor, halting him with a hand to his shoulder as he made to leap for the doors. 'I'm gonna be the first woman on the moon. I know I've been a lot further, but that's amazing. The moon, you never think about it, it's just ... up there. And now I'm on it.' She studied his face. 'I bet you think it's like going to Calais or something.'

The Doctor turned to face her. His features were alive with wonder and excitement. Not for the first time, Rose felt it was as if he was seeing through her eyes, and she wondered if that was one of the reasons he needed somebody to travel with. 'Rose, the moon is incredible. Everything down on Earth relies on it. Rats jump for it. Tides rush out from it. Humans kiss under it. Without it there'd be nothing down there worth the light. And that just happened by chance – trillions of odds against it – one bit of stardust meets another bit of stardust.'

Rose jumped over to the doors and reached out for the handle, then stopped. 'I should think up something to say.'

'Just get out there,' said the Doctor, swinging a bag full of golf clubs on to his shoulder. 'Leap!'

Rose shut her eyes, pulled the door open and leapt.

She came down with a loud thud, smashing into a wooden table. It had been an ordinary leap, not weightless at all.

Picking herself up – the suit's padding had protected her from the worst of the fall – she looked around. There were more tables, stools and chairs, a couple of fruit machines, a blackboard with QUIZ TUESDAYS 8 p.m. TODAY'S SPECIAL CHICKEN CURRY chalked on it, and a long bar with towels over the pumps. All this was lit by the early morning sunlight of a half-hearted early British summer. The building was old, supported by wooden beams.

She turned to face the TARDIS, which stood even more out of place than usual at a corner of the bar. The space-suited Doctor stood in the doors, looking anywhere but at her. 'Wow,' he said. 'Somebody's built an exact replica of a pub on the moon!'

Rose laughed, undid her helmet and pretended to punch him. 'Give it up! You're so rubbish.'

'Not that far out,' said the Doctor a little unhappily, pulling off his own helmet. 'If the moon is Calais, Earth's Dover.' He frowned. 'It's weird, though. I checked all the controls as we were coming in and we were definitely heading for the moon. I even clocked it on the scanner just before we landed, all grey and dusty, the moony old moon, that little old matchmaker in the sky.'

Rose could tell he was really concerned, that this wasn't just an excuse cooked up for her benefit. 'Go and check the TARDIS, then.'

The Doctor nodded. 'I'll go and check the TARDIS, then.' But he stopped at the doors, looking out of the nearest window on to a village green and church that were almost too typical of their kind. 'Looks like May. Looks like

5

England.' He sniffed. 'Not too far from the sea. Hmm, get a whiff of that salt water ...'

Rose laughed and pointed to the TARDIS. 'Go on, go and check it.'

The Doctor picked up his flagpole and bag of golf clubs and vanished back inside the TARDIS.

Rose was about to follow him when she saw a newspaper lying on the bar. She couldn't stop herself from grabbing it in her gloved hand and taking a look, checking the date. The Doctor was right: it was May.

Whenever she came back to Earth, Rose liked to catch up on the news. This was only a local paper, the front page concerned with nothing more exciting than a dispute over parking and a plan for a supermarket, but something made Rose take off her gloves and flick through its pages all the same as she walked idly towards the TARDIS.

A few pages in she stopped dead. She felt her heart miss a beat.

The headline ran ROMAN REMAINS AT CREDITON VALE. Beneath it was a colour picture of a middle-aged man in hard hat and yellow jacket, standing next to a large case that contained a broken section of Roman mosaic about six feet across. Depicted on the mosaic was a full-length portrait of a man and woman, both handsome, dark and curly-haired, in purple robes. Further along were a jug and a bunch of green grapes. And right at the far side, shown in shades of gold on tiny pieces of tile, was a familiar pepperpot shape. Three rods stuck out from it: an eye-stalk from the dome of its head, a sucker attachment and a gun from its middle. Its lower half was studded with shining circular shapes.

A Dalek.

Rose ran for the TARDIS – and the police box door slammed shut in her face. There was a loud thump. The light on top began to flash and the ancient engines deep within the craft ground into life.

'Doctor!' Rose called. 'Doctor, what are you doing?'

Five seconds later, the TARDIS was gone. A deep square imprint on the pub's flowery carpet was the only sign it had ever been there.

CHAPTER TWO

KATE YATES JUST *knew* it was going to be a bad day.

She was dreaming that she was back at school. Everybody else in the class was sixteen, while she was twenty-eight, and there were childish sneers and whispers of 'Why's she *still* here?' Then she heard her dad shouting up the stairs, 'It's eight o'clock!' At the same moment the radio on her bedside table came to life. A few seconds later she heard the front door slam as her parents left for their jobs.

Then the news finished and Wogan began talking, the gentle Irish chatter Kate had known since childhood seeping into her very bones. He talked about toothpaste, last night's TV ... small, funny things. But for Kate he was simply saying, *Just five minutes longer. Five minutes longer in your bed, Kate Yates, in the softest, most comfortable bed in the whole world.*

He stopped talking and played some music.

'This is Anne Murray, "Snowbird".'

Kate knew it was deadly, a song designed specifically to stop people getting out of bed and going to work. It was a drowsy, yawny song. But she couldn't resist, and she turned her face into a deep fold of pillow, closed her eyes and felt that, like the snowbird, she too should spread her tiny wings and fly away.

A second later she heard another voice. A Scottish voice. Ken Bruce. Wogan was handing over to Ken Bruce – which could only mean it wasn't a second later but half past nine.

Kate sat up in bed and checked the clock. 'What?' she screamed. 'How *can* it be? What happened to those ninety minutes?'

She threw back her duvet and ran for the bathroom, tore off her pyjamas, rolled a deodorant under her arms, grabbed a creased blouse from the airing cupboard, slipped into her work skirt and shoes, and hurtled down-stairs. A letter lay on the mat for her: another credit card statement that she could add to the tear-stained folder under her bed. She threw it over her shoulder, grabbed her bag, stuffed half a croissant her mum had left on the phone table into her mouth, and bolted through the front door, into what was often described as one of the most beautiful villages in the UK. But for Kate, Winchelham was only a beautiful trap.

Because she was twenty-eight and back. Back in the room she'd grown up in, waking each morning in the same single bed where, as a teenager, she'd dreamed of leaving. Creeping round the village for fear of bumping into someone from school and having to explain why she was here. The girl with the big-city dreams, returned from London under a cloud of debt, living with her mum and dad. Sorting her life out while working in a call centre by the nature reserve, at a corner desk facing away from the curlews and kingfishers, with a view on to some rubbish bins and the car park.

Thoughts of the call centre quickened Kate's pace down the winding street towards the green. Her boss, Serena, would right now be looking at the empty corner desk, pulling her cardigan over her enormous, unforgiving breasts and tutting. Serena, who wouldn't open filing cabinets in case she broke her nails. Serena, who disapproved of Kate's personal calls, yet seemed to spend half her working day ringing her friend Sheila to discuss her wayward

11

husband in a flat, dull tone. 'I said, "If she's out of your bed and out of your life, how come there are two tickets to the Gambia in your dresser drawer?"'

Calls came from people across the country, furious that their beds hadn't been delivered as promised, or had turned up with no headboard or without wheels. Those calls would now be going to voicemail.

Kate couldn't believe she was actually running *towards* Serena, running *towards* the angry voices.

The village she knew in every detail – every lamp-post, every dodgy paving stone, every litter bin mocking her screwed-up life – blurred past her as she ran to the green and the 9.40 bus. It was now 9.39. The buses were always late, but Kate just knew that this particular bus would be turning the corner by the church exactly on time, about now. That would mean a long walk to work along a shady, muddy lane.

So she ran even faster.

Rose climbed out of her spacesuit. She could hear sounds of movement coming from upstairs. The last thing she wanted right now was to have to explain herself to the landlord, so she unlocked a window, hauled it open and squeezed herself through the gap on to the sunny, empty village street.

She knew the Doctor wouldn't have abandoned her willingly. He'd be back soon with some bizarre and technical explanation. But then she thought of the Dalek on the mosaic. Surely there had to be some connection between it and the Doctor's sudden disappearance ...

She was distracted from these dark thoughts by the prettiness of what lay before her. The clouds were moving away now and the light blue May sky framed an idyllic scene: post office, a little museum, village green and church. The Doctor had been right – beyond the church and over some low hills she caught a glimpse of the sea. A single-decker bus pulled round the corner of the green by the church and drove slowly along. It seemed impossible that the Doctor's hectic, dangerous life could affect such a place, where things were carrying on much as they had for hundreds of years.

Rose sat on a bench and took the TARDIS key from the pocket of her jeans, waiting for it to glow and alert her to the Doctor's return. In the distance she heard the sound of high heels running. Someone was in a hurry.

Kate whizzed round the corner on to the village green as she had done a million times before, sending a rinsed milk bottle left by somebody's front gate flying. She could hear the bus's engine off to the left and knew in her heart she was too late, but still she kept running.

A big ball of bitterness, caused only partly by the croissant she had just eaten, formed in her stomach. Was this it? A year ago she'd been in London, selling her flip-flops in Camden Market, so confident about repaying her business loan to the bank that she was using her credit card to pay her rent. She'd thought she was just getting started. What if she'd already finished, had crashed and burnt? What if she was just useless? What if life was useless?

She saw the back of the bus, on the other side of the green by the pub, rolling smugly away. She crashed to a halt in the middle of the road. A fraction of a second later a bright red sports car zoomed round the corner and smashed into her.

She had one tiny moment to realise that she

was about to die. The credit card bill was never going to be paid off. She would never walk down the long muddy lane in heels, catkins catching on her jacket. Serena would never tell her off for being two hours late. She'd never get to do any of the wonderful things she'd planned. This was the end of it all. A stupid, silly accident.

She thumped down on to the hard tarmac as the car screeched to a halt. The milk bottle jingled by.

The dull smack of metal on flesh caught at Rose's heart. There was no other sound like it – like a soul leaving the body. Her head full of thoughts of her dad, she sprang from the bench and raced across the green.

The driver of the sports car was standing, stunned, by the body of a red-haired young woman. 'I didn't see her,' he called to Rose in a dead voice. 'She just ran out and stopped ...'

'Call an ambulance!' shouted Rose.

The driver got out his mobile and started dialling.

Rose knelt by the young woman and took her hand. The woman's eyelids were fluttering.

There might still be a chance. She remembered watching a first aid video from her old job; after an accident, you have to keep the person talking. 'Listen! Talk to me. My name's Rose Tyler. What's your name?'

The woman said faintly, 'Kate ...'

'What's your second name? Kate, what's your surname? Talk to me! Everything's gonna be fine. There's an ambulance coming.'

Rose clenched the hand in hers, but the middle of Kate's body was horribly twisted, and a deep purple stain of blood was colouring her blouse.

Rose squeezed her hand hard, so hard it hurt. 'Kate!'

Her eyes rolled. 'Yates ... I'm Kate Yates ...' Then Rose saw the light go out of her eyes.

Suddenly something stung Rose's hand. She flinched and drew it back. At the same time, Kate's body twitched and shook. Her back arched. A green aura spread out from the wound, rolling out to cover her whole body. Rose swallowed. The air around Kate had the tang of a thunderstorm; she was crackling with power.

The aura disappeared as quickly as it had

come, as if flicked off by a switch.

Kate's red hair was now blonde.

Rose leaned forward. 'Kate?'

Her blouse still stained, Kate calmly stood and picked up her bag. Rose looked down at where she'd lain, at the pool of fresh blood.

'It's all right, thanks. I'm fine,' said Kate.

CHAPTER THREE

THE DOCTOR LOOKED UP at the grinding central
column of the TARDIS. As soon as he'd touched
the controls, the doors had shut and the craft
had decided to take off. 'Hello! There should be
two passengers on this ship!' he cried.

He crossed to the scanner screen, which was
filled with a strange set of symbols he hadn't
seen before. He knew one thing for sure,
though: the TARDIS was not under the control
of an outside influence. It had changed course
from the moon and brought them to Earth.
Now it was taking him somewhere else. Even
after nine centuries of travel through space and
time, it could still surprise him.

'What are you trying to tell me? Don't go all
cryptic. Can't you just *say*? And where are we
going now – Northampton?' He flicked a few
buttons with no result. 'Stop, stop!'

A second later the column shuddered to a
halt, the big room tilting and knocking him off

his feet. He switched the screen to an outside view of his new location. It showed a dark, empty concrete chamber. He stripped off his spacesuit and took his pinstripe suit jacket from a peg. Putting it on, he grabbed a torch from a locker, then swung the doors open and strode out. Wherever the TARDIS had taken him, and for whatever reason, it had only been in flight for a few seconds. He couldn't be very far from where he'd left Rose.

It certainly looked and smelt very different from the last stop. The air was damp and decayed, with that special flat coolness you only find underground. The beam of his torch pierced through the pitch blackness. It passed over bare concrete pillars to settle on a metal sign with AREA 3 written on it in stark, official lettering. Next to it was a bracket where a fire extinguisher would once have fitted.

Beside that was a huge studded dark green metal door, swung wide open. He walked through it into a long, bare corridor. 'Hello. Anyone about?' he called, not expecting an answer. The place seemed deserted, abandoned.

He walked a little further down the corridor and turned into another room. The torch lit up two lines of old, rusting iron beds. On the wall by the door was a phone; the Doctor lifted it and listened. It was dead. The sole of his shoe scuffed against something on the floor. He knelt down and picked up a tattered booklet with the title 'Protect and Survive' and a date of 1980. ' "Eat only tinned food," ' he read from it. ' "If you live in a caravan or other similar accommodation which provides very little protection against fall-out, your local authority will be able to advise you on what to do." ' He laughed to himself. 'Hello. It's the council and we advise you to run like hell.'

So he was in a nuclear bunker, a disused one by the look of it. But why had the TARDIS brought him here?

Before he had time to think about it any further, he heard something he was not expecting. He strained to listen. Yes, he was right. Somebody, somewhere in this bunker, was listening to the radio.

He set off in search of that person.

Frank Openshaw sat back proudly in his chair, watching the dig, tapping his toes to the song on the radio. The slow, patient business of his greatest project yet was spread out before him. Volunteers, mostly students from the local farming college, were working carefully down in the pit, which was lit by several huge lamps. He took a swig of coffee from the cup of his thermos flask, feeling secure and successful. This site was going to make his name. He didn't care too much about the fame, but the security of guaranteed work was another matter. He'd never let Sandra down again.

Somebody tapped him on the shoulder. 'Excuse me, can I borrow your phone?' asked a voice in a slightly odd, London-but-not-quite-London accent.

Frank looked up. The owner of the voice was too old to be a student; he was tall and very thin, dark-haired, dressed in a slightly scruffy suit. Frank blinked. It was as if someone had switched on a bright light. The stranger shone with confidence and enthusiasm, and he found himself handing over his mobile phone without even thinking about it.

'You won't get a signal down here,' Frank warned him.

'Bet I will,' said the stranger. He took a slender metal tube from his pocket, flicked a switch on its side and held its tip to the side of the phone. Then he dialled.

Frank looked on fascinated.

He heard a woman's voice on the phone. 'OK, what happened?'

'I'm blaming the TARDIS,' said the stranger. 'Yeah, it's all the TARDIS's fault. It's got all these emergency systems. I turned them all off years ago. They kept going off and I couldn't hear myself think. Must have come back on. I'm at –' he looked at Frank – 'Where am I?'

'Crediton Vale,' said Frank.

'Crediton Vale, disused bunker, must be about a mile and a half away. Lovely walk for you. I'm jealous. See you in a bit.'

'Hold on, Doctor,' said the woman's voice urgently. 'Something really weird and important. Two things actually. First, there's this dig, and they've –'

'Yeah, I'm there now. See you later. I can't talk because I'm on someone else's phone.' He snapped the phone shut and handed it back to Frank. Then he rubbed his hands and looked down into the pit. 'Digging,' he said. 'Don't know if I like digging. Digging can be good, digging can be bad. Depending on what the diggers are digging up.' He turned to Frank and gave a wide, wide smile. 'I know. Shall I stop talking for a bit?'

Frank was looking at his phone's screen. No bars. 'The signal's gone,' he said.

'Has it?' replied the stranger innocently.

Frank pointed to the metal tube in the stranger's hand. 'What's that? How did it do that?'

'Don't ask me,' said the stranger. 'Birthday present from my sister-in-law. I wanted a tie.' He pointed over Frank's shoulder to a long piece of rotted wood, one of their biggest finds so far, which was tagged and laid out on a long work table. 'That's the turning spike from a Roman well, about AD 70. Tie your horse there, round and round it goes. Five minutes later one nice bucket of water, one very dizzy horse.'

Frank got up and followed him to the table, scratching his head. 'I thought it was a supporting beam,' he said. Something about this bloke made him feel like a beginner.

'No, look at the edges. Too smooth for that.' He reached out and shook Frank's hand very tightly. 'I'm the Doctor, by the way.'

'Frank Openshaw. They said someone was coming down from London ...'

'Did they?' The Doctor saw another find on the table, a worn Roman coin. 'Ah, look at that. Nero. Takes me back.' He knelt, slipped on a pair of glasses and chuckled at the man's profile on the coin. 'He was fatter than that.' He pointed upwards. 'So, there was a Roman town there, right? And it went up in the revolt of Boudicca. The Britons chucked everything down into these caves. About 1950 the British government builds a great big bunker in the caves: centre of regional government. Looks like a bungalow up top, very secret. When the Cold War ends, someone goes to fill this place in and build some flats on the surface. Then they find this stuff and call you in. Am I right or what?'

Frank swallowed. 'Pretty much. OK, come and have a look at this.' He led the Doctor to the pile of most recent finds and handed him a metal triangle. 'Gardening tool?'

The Doctor shook his head sadly. 'No, handle's wrong. That's a pizza slice. Except they didn't have tomatoes then. It was more like herby cheese on toast. Cheesy naan actually.

25

Yum.' He took off his glasses, put them away and looked right at Frank. 'Sorry. Am I being annoying?'

'Didn't catch your name,' said Frank.

'Just the Doctor. The. Doctor.' He scratched the back of his neck. 'Now, would I be wrong to think you've dug something up that you really, really don't understand?'

Frank sighed. 'And I suppose you'll know just what it is.'

The Doctor shrugged. 'Might do. Sorry. Everybody loves a smartarse ...'

Frank pointed down a narrow corridor that led off the main dig. 'Image on the right of the mosaic. Down there. Follow the lights.'

The Doctor gave him a thumbs-up and walked off. Frank stared after him and wondered. And the more he wondered, the odder the thoughts that came into his head.

One of the students broke into his thinking. 'Frank!' he called from the pit. 'There's something metal down here. Dead weird it is!'

The Doctor sauntered along the corridor. A standard lamp shone down on to a display case with a large, rough-edged mosaic inside. The

Doctor guessed that when the Britons had looted the Roman town above, they'd tossed it down into the caves too.

He saw what was depicted there and felt his hearts skip a beat. At the same moment he heard cries of excitement and surprise from the main dig. The radio was switched off.

He ran back. 'Frank! Mr Openshaw!'

He emerged into the huge hollowed-out room and jumped down into the pit, striding over to where Openshaw and his workers were gathered in a far corner.

'Get away from it!' he called, pushing a couple of the students aside.

And found himself facing a Dalek.

CHAPTER FOUR

'Looks like a robot,' said Frank.

The thing had been unearthed hurriedly by the students. In their excitement they had forgotten that the first rule of archaeology was patience. Its base was still covered in earth and its sides were caked in lumps of dirt. It looked exactly like the thing in the mosaic. Its golden casing had lost its colour but it remained whole. Eye-stalk, sucker and stubby gun were lifted arrogantly. The Doctor waved a hand over the eyepiece. No reaction.

He seemed to consider for a second. Then, as Frank moved to touch it, he cried, 'It's a bomb! Step back from it, Frank!'

Frank pulled his hand back. One of the students looked the Doctor up and down, then asked, 'Who's this?'

Frank and the Doctor looked at each other. Somehow, Frank trusted this odd young stranger. 'It's the bloke from London,' he heard himself saying, though he knew it wasn't true.

The Doctor slapped the student's arm down as he lifted it towards the gun stick. 'And the bloke from London says get back!' Then he grabbed a loud hailer from the floor of the pit and called, 'Evacuate the area! I have authority from London and all that! Get up to the surface now!'

Frank wasn't surprised when the students obeyed. But he found himself remaining.

The museum teashop opened early. Kate, who was the only customer, munched in a daze on a teacake while speaking on the phone to Serena. Getting angry with Serena was pointless – but still, Kate was getting angry. 'Yes, I was nearly run over. Just now.'

'Nearly run over running for the late bus, then?' asked Serena's dull, flat voice.

'The "nearly run over" part of the sentence is the important bit!' Kate snapped.

She felt a wave of anger rushing up inside her. Why did she have to even *pretend* to be polite to this idiot? The meaning of the phrase 'seeing red' suddenly became clear to her. She felt that if Serena had been there she could have picked up her butter knife and stabbed her. But she wasn't, so she flipped her mobile shut and grabbed the café's copy of the paper from the counter. Idly, she turned to the puzzle page. She might have a go at the easy crossword to calm herself down.

The sudoku puzzles caught her eye instead. She'd hardly bothered to look at them before – she'd always been rubbish at maths – but this morning the numbers seemed to dance in the air. Without even thinking about it she filled all the empty boxes in – for all three: the easy, hard and killer sudokus – her fingers whizzing across the page. Then she looked at the crosswords. She filled in the blanks with letters easily, solving even the hardest clues in fractions of a second.

It was easy. Really easy. Why had she never noticed that before?

She looked around, taking deep breaths. Something in the world had changed – or was it inside her?

She could see the atoms dancing around the room. She knew the exact temperature of her coffee. She saw and understood the chemical processes taking place inside the cup. But this wasn't like thinking. She didn't have to concentrate, or make an effort. It felt as natural as breathing. And with it came a sense of strength and power. Her hand reached for a sachet of sweetener in a bowl. She rubbed it gently between her thumb and finger and watched as it broke apart in a little blizzard of static electricity.

She took another deep breath and looked up. Someone had entered the little shop – the pretty blonde girl who'd held her hand out in the road, Rose. That seemed like a dream. She wanted to sneer. As if a speeding car could stop *her*!

'So you're OK now?' asked Rose.

Kate smiled. 'I'm fine, thanks. Just gonna finish this and go to work. Thanks.'

Rose sat down next to her, leaning close. 'That car smacked right into you. You were dying. What's the deal? You can tell me.'

Kate bridled. 'Sorry. Could you move a bit back? I like my personal space.'

Rose pointed to Kate's blouse. 'You're covered in blood. You should be dead.'

There was something very kind and trusting in the girl's deep brown eyes. Kate swallowed;

a cruel thought came into her mind. Such emotions were *weak*.

Rose went on, 'I know what it feels like. Something happens that you can't explain. You invent any excuse to stop thinking about it.'

'What's your name again?' asked Kate, though she knew.

'Rose. Rose Tyler.' She held out her hand.

Kate took it, shook it. Tight. 'Great. Now then, Rose Tyler, clear off. I've got enough on my plate.'

Rose flinched and pulled her hand away.

Frank watched as the Doctor ran that glowing metal tube of his slowly over the object he'd described as a bomb. Then the Doctor gave a deep sigh. Some of the cheeky light came back into his eyes. He looked across at Frank. 'Is there any point me asking you to go home?'

'None,' said Frank. He pointed to the section of the bomb where the domed head met a rusty metal grille surrounded by metal slats. 'Could be a hinge there.'

The Doctor smiled. 'I like you, Frank Openshaw. You're clever.'

He applied the tip of the tube to the hinge and

then carefully lifted up the dome. Frank came closer. Inside there was a tangle of electronic parts and wires. It looked as if something was missing in this central space, something about the size of a football that would once have sat there. The Doctor reached in and picked up a handful of dust. He sifted it between his fingers and then blew it away.

'Dead as a doornail,' he said. He seemed relieved – but also, Frank felt, perhaps a little sad, as if staring into the past.

Frank made a small snorting noise. 'A bomb? In earth that hasn't been touched for 2,000 years?'

The Doctor rubbed the dust from his hands and smiled. 'OK, clever Frank Openshaw, you've got me. It's not strictly a bomb.' He patted the casing. 'It's all that's left of the most terrifying thing in the universe.'

'I've never seen one before,' said Frank.

'And you don't how lucky you are.' He whistled and pointed over his shoulder with his thumb. 'Now really, hop it.' He returned to his study of the object.

Frank didn't move. He considered the Doctor's words. 'You said "universe".'

'What about it?' asked the Doctor.

'Nobody would say "the most terrifying thing in the universe". Unless they were mad, and you're not mad.'

The Doctor frowned. 'Go home, Frank. You've got a day off. Put your feet up, have sausage and chips, watch *Brainteaser*. Come back tomorrow.'

'You'd only say "universe" if you were – I don't know, from space,' said Frank, laughing to himself as he said it.

The Doctor blinked. 'Don't be silly.'

Frank pointed to the object. 'And that could be from space too. And from what you said about Nero, and the pizza ... you'd only know that if you'd been there.' He laughed once more at the madness of what he was saying.

The Doctor blinked again. For once he wasn't saying anything.

'Sorry. Am I being annoying?' asked Frank. He knew his theory couldn't be true.

The Doctor laughed and clapped him around the shoulders. 'No. Now, I really, *really* like you.' He pointed to the object. 'That's a Dalek. No – that *was* a Dalek. From the planet Skaro. Once, yeah, the most terrifying things in the universe. They were very gifted at war. Now they're all dead, all the creatures inside. This is just the shell, a heap of old bits. There's more life in a tramp's vest!'

It was the strangest conversation of Frank's life. The Doctor was obviously joking, making all this up, but still Frank decided to join in. 'So what killed them?' he asked.

'I did,' said the Doctor. 'Many battles, one final war.' He kicked the base of the Dalek. 'There's nothing to be scared of any longer.'

'I want you to meet a mate of mine,' said Rose, trailing Kate as she left the teashop. 'He can help you.'

Kate sighed. 'Thank you for your concern, but I really am fine.'

Rose grabbed her by the shoulder and turned her to face one of the museum's windows. 'You're blonde. When you ran out in the road, I saw you. You had curly red hair, and now ... look!'

Kate saw herself in the window. Her hair was straight and bright yellow, like some Swedish supermodel's. She shuddered, took a step back. She couldn't accept what she saw.

'Kate, come and meet the Doctor,' said Rose.

Kate's head swivelled round. The movement felt totally instinctive. *Doctor! The Doctor!*

'Come on,' said Rose, taking her gently by the hand. 'He's at a place called Crediton Vale. Do you know that?'

Kate nodded. Another bus was just turning on to the green. She pointed. 'We can get that and be there in five minutes.'

'Don't be scared. He'll know what to do,' said Rose, leading her to the bus stop.

As she walked across the peaceful village street of her childhood, terrible images ran through Kate's mind's eye. Somebody else's memories. Whole worlds burning, planets falling through space like balls scattered over a snooker table. The word *Doctor* echoed in her head. She saw the shadow shape of a man framed by fire. There was a knot of anger inside her, something vicious and confident and sharp. Then another emotion took over – fear.

A word started running through her head. Its four syllables demanded to be shouted out loud, again and again.

Exterminate!

CHAPTER FIVE

THE DOCTOR GENTLY LOOSENED the connections and removed the Dalek gun an inch at a time.

Frank noted that there was sweat on his brow. 'Thought it wasn't dangerous,' he said.

'Not in itself,' said the Doctor, holding the gun at arm's length. 'But you tell me, what happens if some clever clogs gets this in his lab? Finds out how it works? The human race gets the secret of Dalek weapons. You'll all be dead by Wednesday week.'

He placed the weapon with care into Frank's hands, rolled up his sleeves and bent over the open casing, using the metal tube to work inside.

Frank looked down at the weapon, confused. Part of him didn't believe a word of what the Doctor was saying. But the other part of him believed every bit of it.

A few moments later, the Doctor looked up and said, 'Frank, you don't ask questions.

Normally by now people are saying, "What's it like in space? Can I go back and save Kennedy? Can I stop myself meeting the wife?" That sort of thing.'

Frank nodded to the Dalek. 'That looks tricky. Don't want to put you off.' He smiled. 'And I love my wife,' he added sincerely. 'If I could go back, change anything, I'd want to meet her years before I did. Funny, she was in her third year at Durham University when I was in my first year, but we never met for another ten years.'

The Doctor stood up straight. 'You are a remarkable person. Right. I need to ask you something.' He tapped the Dalek. 'I'm taking this to bits. Just for safe keeping, take the gun away. Pretty soon, someone up there's gonna come down here and start asking questions.' He nodded to the gun. 'They can get their hands on me, OK, but nobody must get their hands on that. Pop it in your bag and take it home. I'll pick it up this evening.'

Frank's bag was made of faded green canvas. He'd had it since the 1970s. He picked it up and put the Dalek weapon inside, next to his lunchbox and paper.

'What's your postcode?' asked the Doctor.

'WP4 2LN,' said Frank.

The Doctor thought for a second. 'Redlands Road, Twyford?'

Frank felt even more confused now, but eventually he simply shook his head and smiled. 'That's it, number 15. I'll see you later, then.' He set off for the exit.

As he was nearing the huge lift, the Doctor called, 'Frank.' Frank turned. 'Can't do that thing with the wife. It bends the rules. But ... I could manage the fall of Troy from a safe distance?'

Frank shrugged. It was like a game of bluff, he half-decided. The Doctor was just being silly. 'Ta. But I'm happy where I am, Doctor.' He entered the lift and pressed the button to go up.

Kate and Rose got off the bus at what looked like a building site. A series of half-built flats lay across a field beyond a high wire fence. Cranes with various attachments were dotted around the site, along with piles of building materials. About a quarter of a mile beyond was the sea, radiant and blue, on what was turning out to be a warm day for May. A security man and a bunch of people who looked like students were standing outside a bungalow in the middle of the site. Voices were being raised.

Kate pointed to the bungalow. 'That's the entrance to the bunker. It was a bit of a tourist attraction. Then they decided to fill it in.' As she spoke, a middle-aged man carrying an old canvas bag walked by. Kate eyed him with interest, not knowing why. Her skin tingled with static.

Rose nodded at the fuss by the bungalow. 'Oh yeah, the Doctor's definitely down there. People are shouting. Come on.'

She led Kate over the rough ground. They waited until the security man, who was in the middle of the students, looked the other way, then slipped into the old bungalow. Inside was a huge iron lift, its doors open. They got in and Rose pressed the button to go down.

Kate looked over at Rose. 'I suppose I don't mind going blonde.'

'It's not so bad,' said Rose.

'Naturally blonde,' said Kate.

It was the kind of friendly, mock-bitchy thing she'd say all the time. But inside, her mind was stirring with visions she couldn't even find words to describe. She knew she must keep them secret. Keeping secrets and lying had never appealed to her before. She remembered an ex telling her – in the process of him becoming an ex – that one of her most annoying qualities was that she always showed her real feelings. Today, being cunning felt like a thrill. She could tell this Rose anything, and then, when the time came, when Rose trusted her the most, she would turn – and exterminate her!

The lift jolted and Rose ran out into a huge pit. A skinny man in a slightly crumpled suit was bending over something on the far side. Rose ran across to him. 'Doctor! On this mosaic, there's a –'

The skinny man turned, revealing what he'd been looking at. Kate felt a thrill run through her. The man was nothing like the shadowy shape she'd seen in the visions, but she knew somehow that he was the same person.

And the object he'd been looking at – it uplifted her, called to her. She longed to run towards it, embrace it, but she knew the Doctor was dangerous. This game would have to be played with that wonderful cunning.

Rose had stopped dead at the sight of it. 'It's impossible. They all died.'

The Doctor came towards her, took her arm. 'Yeah. They all did. Even this one. Dead. Like all the others.'

Kate felt she had to say something. 'What is it?' she asked, trying her best to appear dumb and ordinary.

The Doctor looked her over. 'Oh, great, we're back to the questions. Knew that wouldn't last.' He turned to Rose. 'Who is this?'

Rose couldn't take her eyes off the object. 'You sure it's dead?'

'Are you?' he asked gently. 'You looked into the time vortex. You used its power. You destroyed them all. You're not saying you missed a bit?'

Rose blinked, as if she was trying to remember something hidden from her. Then she smiled. 'No, I got them all. And I'm not sorry I did.'

'So,' said the Doctor. 'Your friend ...?'

He nodded over to Kate. Kate nodded back. The part of her that was still Kate found him rather attractive.

'Yeah,' said Rose. 'She's called Kate. And

there's something else, something really weird about her.'

The Doctor nodded. 'Nice to meet you, Kate.' Then he turned back to Rose, ignoring her. 'Rose, I've got one chance to do this. I've got to take it to bits, then we'll dump it somewhere. There's a lovely black hole in the galaxy Casta Pizellus that'll do very nicely. I can't risk taking it into the TARDIS intact.'

'It's dead, though,' said Rose. 'Isn't it?'

'There's an old saying,' said the Doctor, 'dates from about 4000: "Never turn your back on a dead Dalek." The casings were full of booby traps. There's a slight chance there are still virus transmitters in the shell. They could latch on to the TARDIS's power systems.'

'What, and bring it back to life?'

'No, but they could take over the TARDIS computer. Like nasty computer viruses. Less than a chance in a trillion. But, come on, with our luck are we gonna risk that?'

Rose looked back at Kate. 'But –'

'Please. Five minutes and I'll be finished. It can't be as important as this.'

He walked back to the thing – Dalek, he had called it. Kate had never heard that word before, but it caused a deep feeling of satisfaction within her strange new mind.

As the Doctor ran a long metal tube inside the casing and chattered on to Rose, Kate walked round slowly to the other side. She put on an innocent, curious face.

'Must have crashed and burnt here thousands of years ago, fleeing the Time War,' the Doctor was telling Rose. 'The Romans dug it up, put it on show in their villa. An antique, something to talk about at dinner parties. "Peel me a grape, Marcus, and have a look at what I've got." Then it got thrown down here. And today someone digs it up again.'

'After that long, how could a computer virus or whatever survive?' asked Rose.

'Probably all wiped out when it crashed,' said the Doctor. 'But I know about Daleks. They always, *always* had something you never knew about ...'

He looked up to see Kate reaching out, stretching her fingers into the casing, reaching for the spaghetti-like mass of connections.

Tiny glowing filaments, like strands of sparkling green glue, were flowing from her fingertips into the Dalek.

CHAPTER SIX

THE DOCTOR PUT HIS HEAD down and charged at Kate like a bull, knocking her to the ground beneath him.

Rose stared at the Dalek casing, instinctively backing away. A faint green glow remained, shining up from the empty main section. 'What's she done?'

The Doctor got up and smacked his fist against his forehead, hard. 'Why didn't I listen to you? Tell me everything!'

So Rose quickly told him the story of Kate's incredible recovery from the accident, all the while watching the dying glow in the Dalek and worrying.

Kate was shaking with fear. The Doctor raised her hand carefully and felt her fingers. 'Static! There's some kind of Dalek energy inside her.'

'But she's human,' said Rose.

'They had a gift for war. New weapons every other day. She was trying to make the machinery in the casing work again. Even without a Dalek inside, the shell is dangerous. It could run on automatic, like a chicken with its head cut off.'

Kate blinked and looked round, confused. 'What's happened to me?' she managed to say.

'You'll be all right,' said the Doctor, but with a confidence Rose had learned to mistrust slightly. 'She's a new weapon.'

'But how?' Rose pointed to the Dalek. 'It's dead!'

The Doctor was thinking. 'And what if, when it was dying, it sent something out, a genetic imprint? Remember that the Daleks hate the human race. They loathe all other creatures. Why would they even consider mixing their race with another? No mixed marriages for Daleks.' He shook his head. 'Perhaps they imprinted the Dalek factor in the human race, or tried to. Why?' He indicated Kate. 'And thousands of years later, the imprint's still there, buried away in her genes. Something triggered it off today, so she gets strength, intelligence, the power to heal herself.'

The Doctor helped Kate to her feet and steered her away from the Dalek.

Another terrifying thought struck Rose. 'The Dalek factor,' she whispered. 'It could be in me? In everyone?'

'No. This must be a fluke. Whatever the plan was, it went wrong. The Dalek got killed. The imprint failed.'

'How do you know?'

'If they'd passed the Dalek factor on to the whole of humanity, I think I'd have noticed.' He handed Kate gently over to Rose. 'We've got to get her away, far away. I'll sort it out later. There'll be a way. The further she gets, the safer she'll be. What's she called again?'

'Kate Yates.'

'Cruel parents and the Dalek factor. Unlucky girl. Go!'

Rose grabbed Kate round the middle and ran for the lift as fast as possible.

The Doctor returned to the Dalek casing. The green sparkles had faded.

The electronics inside were damaged by age. It was unlikely that Kate had managed to spark them into life, but it was worth making certain.

He waited, thinking over his next move. After

a minute, he raised the sonic screwdriver for another check and peered inside.

A greasy green eye blinked up at him. A newly formed Dalek creature, smaller than an adult, was already stretching its slime-coated tentacles towards the connections.

The Doctor leapt back. 'No,' he breathed, staggering a little. 'No. That's impossible ...'

He hesitated for a second. He knew he had to kill it – and kill it *now*. Could he?

The casing slammed shut on its hinge with a deafening clang.

The tip of the eye-stalk opened, glowing a bright, healthy blue.

The sucker arm started to twitch. The base shifted, freeing itself from the earth that covered it. A croak came from the grating beneath the head. '*Aaaaaa ...*'

The lights on the domed head flickered into life.

The Doctor realised that he had one option left, an option that had served him well on many occasions. He ran to the lift doors and pressed the up button desperately.

Over his shoulder, the Dalek was slowly turning its eye-stalk and sucker arm, moving unsteadily from side to side on its base.

The Doctor kicked the lift doors. 'Come on!'

He heard the lift settle into position, saw the doors open, ran inside and pushed the up button. The lift doors closed with casual slowness. Just before they closed completely, the Doctor saw the Dalek moving over the uneven ground of the pit towards him, its base a few inches off the ground.

The lift started going up.

The Dalek reached the closed door of the lift shaft. The socket where its gun had been twitched uselessly. Then its sucker arm reached out to the thick steel where the doors met, forming a cup against it. It tugged.

The doors bulged out. The Dalek pulled at the huge chunk of metal until it was free, then tossed it aside with ease.

It darted into the lift shaft, switched into its anti-gravity mode and started to rise.

The lift was moving up with, it seemed to the Doctor, painful slowness. He heard a couple of shattering crashes from deep below him and thumped the wall. 'Come on, come *on* ...'

*

The Dalek rose up the shaft. Its eye turned to the base of the climbing lift. Its young mind considered.

Slowly it tilted itself backwards. Then its sucker arm extended from the casing. It clamped on to the base of the lift with a metallic clang.

It heaved. Gears crunched and the motor screamed. The Dalek began to drag the lift – and the Doctor – back down.

CHAPTER SEVEN

THE LIFT JUDDERED. Gears screeched.

The Doctor looked up. The ceiling of the lift was made up of four metal plates. He stretched to his fullest height and aimed the sonic screwdriver at them, loosening the massive bolts in the corners. He heard the bolts fall one by one and slide across the floor of the lift.

He steadied himself, then spat on his hands and leapt, knocking the roof of the lift, trying to push one of the panels off to the side. It barely moved.

Below him, he could hear the newborn Dalek croaking.

He took another jump, bashing his palms against the panel. It shifted slightly.

Something rammed into the base of the lift. He looked down. A hole was being ripped in the floor.

Using all his strength, the Doctor jumped

again, knocking the panel aside. He jumped a fourth time, gripping the rough edge of the free corner.

The hole in the floor grew bigger as the Dalek's sucker tore at the metal. Though it was young, confused, still forming, the Doctor realised, it must have worked out how to use its sensors to see through into the lift. To see him.

He pulled himself up and out through the gap into the lift shaft, thankful for his skinny frame. Then he grabbed hold of the steel cable and climbed up it, hand over hand.

Rose got Kate out of the site and on to the main road. It was easy to hitch a lift from a passing lorry driver. 'Two blondes,' thought Rose. 'Double hitching power.' She told the driver, a pleasant young man who introduced himself as Atif, that Kate was feeling a little sick. They got up into the cab with him.

Kate's eyes flickered open fully and she turned to Rose. 'What just happened back there?'

'Don't worry about it. We're getting away,' said Rose, trying to sound confident. She turned to Atif. 'Where are you headed?'

'France eventually,' he said. 'I can drop you off in Hastings, Dover ...'

Rose took another look at Kate. 'Dover's fine.'

The Doctor crashed out of the bungalow. He looked quickly round the site, trying to spot any advantage, any tool he could use against the Dalek.

His face fell. 'Oh no.' A couple of police cars had chosen that exact moment to arrive, turning on to the waste ground. A security man and the student diggers were clustered round the site entrance.

One of the students spotted him and pointed. 'That's him, the bloke from London.'

The Doctor raced forward. 'Please, you've all got to get out of here!' He looked back at the bungalow. The noise of tearing metal echoed from inside. 'Now!'

The security man stared at him uncertainly. 'Can I see your identification, please, sir?'

The Doctor felt for his psychic paper, then decided against it. Explaining would just waste time. 'There's no time for that!' he shouted. 'Run! Get out, all of you, now!'

His hearts sank as he saw four police officers

get out of their cars. The students were looking at him, this time with amusement. The security man put a hand on his shoulder.

The Doctor knew what was coming for these innocents and it chilled him.

A gargling croak came from behind and he whipped round. The Dalek was moving across the waste ground towards them, its eye-stalk and sucker arm twisting and turning angrily.

The students laughed nervously. The security man took his hand from the Doctor's shoulder and frowned, trying to understand what he was seeing.

'It's newborn,' said the Doctor quietly. 'It's not fully formed. There's still a chance, but you must all get away now.'

The police officers surrounded him, while at the same time turning confused, half-amused faces towards the Dalek. Their leader addressed the Doctor. 'OK, sir, I think it's time you and your robot left these people to do their job.'

The Dalek moved closer, its eye sweeping over the humans, as if curious.

'Hey, it's got a sink plunger on it!' cried one of the students.

The Dalek croaked angrily and zoomed over

to him. Its sucker arm extended, then shot out and fixed itself to his middle. Then it picked him up and tossed him aside. His body flew through the air, coming down with a crunch of bone and flesh on the hard ground.

That was when everyone started screaming and running.

The Dalek lifted into the air, cutting off their escape through the main gate. Its sucker arm shot out and clamped on to the side of one of the police cars. There was a screeching of twisted metal. The car lurched, bumped, rocked on its tyres. Then slowly, straining and creaking, it started to rise. Just a little at first – high on the suspension. Then it left the ground, the Dalek's terrifying strength holding it. The seats fell forward as it tilted, loose objects flying about inside. The sucker arm suddenly shot out even further and hurled the car forwards. The car flew low across the ground, finally catching on a mound of earth from the dig. It spun, rolled and crashed down, inches from the terrified humans, in an ear-splitting din of glass and tearing metal. Then the petrol caught fire, turning the car into a blazing wreck in seconds and ending any hope of escape.

The Doctor looked on with horror as the Dalek zoomed forwards, forcing the crowd into a narrow alley between two of the flats. 'No! Get out of there!' he cried, running after them.

The Dalek waited until they were all in the alley. Then it followed them, lifted itself up and started to crash between the walls. On top of one wall was a mass of girders and heavy metal scaffolding pipes. The vibrations started to roll them towards the edge. In a few seconds, they would crash down on the huddled, terrified mass of innocent humans.

The Doctor ran forward. 'Oi, Dalek!' he shouted.

The Dalek instantly stopped its battering against the walls. Its domed head section whipped round and its eye focused on the Doctor.

'Da ... lek,' it croaked. 'Da ... lek ...'

'Yeah, I know who you are. I know what you are. And you know something else? Those are just humans. Any passing evil being from space can have a go at them. That's easy. But do you know what I am? Do you know who I am?'

The humans used the Dalek's distraction. They ran out under it as it swooped, as though fascinated, towards the Doctor. Its blue eye zeroed in on him, scanning him up and down.

'You ... are ... not ... hu-man,' it said, each word forming slowly.

The Doctor walked forward casually, trying to give the others time to get away. He flung open his coat and pointed to his chest. 'Give him a biscuit. Take a look at these beauties.'

The Dalek continued its scan. It shook slightly, as if surprised. 'Two ... hearts.'

The Doctor nodded. 'Yes. Aren't you a clever little Dalek? Now, consult your data store. Go on. What does that mean? What does that make me? Come on. I haven't got all day to waste talking to you.' He glanced to one side – the humans were running from the site. Death was on hold, for them at least.

The Dalek's sucker arm shot up. Its weapon socket clicked uselessly. 'You ... are a Time ... Lord!' The final word was spoken with the upward screech the Doctor knew so well.

'And not just any old ten-for-a-penny common-or-garden value-pack Time Lord,' the Doctor teased. 'Do you know who I am?' He leaned forward, almost spitting the words, one by one. 'I am the Doctor!'

The Dalek quivered.

'I'm sorry,' said the Doctor mildly. 'Did that word upset you in some way? Have another look in your data store, boy. I might be in there under *Oncoming Storm, The*.'

'Doc-tor,' the Dalek groaned. Its weapon socket clicked again. '*The* Doc-tor!'

He waved. 'That's me!'

'The Doc-tor is an enemy of the Daleks!'

'Wrong! The Daleks are an enemy of the Doctor. No, strike that, the Daleks *were* an enemy of the Doctor!'

'The Doctor must be exterminated!'

'With what?' The Doctor ran off, with something very particular in mind, leading the Dalek away from the main gate, deeper into the site. 'If you're so hard, come and get me!'

The Dalek zoomed after him.

CHAPTER EIGHT

KATE'S FOREHEAD WAS PRESSED against the window of the driver's cab. She watched the B-roads go by. All the little cars with all the little people inside. They were hateful, inferior forms of life. She saw a child standing up on a back seat to wave at her and she cringed. Why had she never noticed how ugly people were?

There was just no *point* to people. They were wasteful, always at war with each other. They were better off dead, and the universe would be a tidier place without them. The part of her that was still Kate argued, in a small voice, that they were innocent. *No one is innocent!* ranted the Dalek part. These creatures were genetically inferior. Only the Daleks were pure.

A wave of bile washed up into her mouth. She winced, sickened, and the shock allowed the Kate part of her to assert itself.

'You OK?' asked Rose.

Kate looked into her concerned brown eyes.

61

'What's happening to me?' she asked, tears welling. 'I keep thinking disgusting things. There's so much hatred, anger, I feel I could – kill the world, the whole world ...'

She noticed Atif the lorry driver eyeing her oddly. 'I'm always like that on a Thursday,' he called over cheerfully.

A stab of evil pierced her. What a stupid thing to say, what a waste of words.

Rose put her arm round Kate's shoulder. 'Believe in me,' she said. 'I promise you, it's all going to get back to normal.'

'And who are you to promise that?' snapped Kate. 'You're just trying to sound like him.'

'Who?'

'The Doctor,' Kate spat. She struck out with her foot, banging her knee on the underside of the dashboard. 'I know all about him. It's in my head. The destroyer, the oncoming storm. Always blocking our way ...'

'The way to what?'

'Purity. I can see it ... the universe cleansed. So beautiful, serene. Only us, only Daleks.'

'You're not a Dalek,' Rose stressed.

'I will be,' said Kate. 'You don't know how good it's going to be. Peace for ever. No war.'

'But quite a lot of shooting to get there,' said Rose. 'And what are the Daleks gonna do when they've exterminated everyone? Stroll through the meadows in floral skirts, making daisy chains?'

'Do not be flippant.' Kate smiled. 'Daleks working together. Daleks studying together. An ordered empire stretching out for all time. So clean and calm.' She shook her head as if to clear it. 'Like the words of "Imagine". I'd do anything to get there.'

Rose swallowed, looking rather alarmed, and tried to change the subject. 'Kate, who did you last go out with?'

Kate flinched at the memory. 'I went out with an inferior. Toby. He spent my money, and it wasn't even mine to begin with. Because of Toby, I used all the credit on my card. I will find and *exterminate* Toby.' Her fist clenched.

Atif kept shooting worried glances at Kate. 'Is your mate feeling all right?'

'She's fine,' said Rose. She took Kate's hand. 'Come on, Kate. You can fight it.'

Kate pulled her hand away, disgusted. 'Do not put your flesh against me!' she shrieked. 'Human flesh stinks! It is impure!'

'Think I'll make a detour to the hospital, shall I?' said Atif.

Kate leaned over Rose, pinning her against her seat, and grabbed the wheel of the lorry, twisting it violently. The lorry swerved as Atif hit the brakes. It bumped across the road, grinding to a halt on a grass verge next to a row of shops. Kate was pleased to see they had arrived in Twyford, the nearest town. It was nearly lunchtime on market day and it was sunny. The place would be crawling with humans.

Rose grabbed her round the waist, and put her hand in Kate's face. Kate threw her back with a casual flick of her elbow and scrambled out of the lorry. She landed like a cat on the grass, stood and licked her dry lips.

Rose sat up, trying to draw breath. Kate's blow had winded her. She found Atif staring at her, shaking his head, more stunned than angry.

'What's your mate been taking?'

'Drive! Get out of here!' Rose urged him. She threw herself out of the lorry and looked round desperately for Kate.

They were in a small market town, with half-timbered buildings leading off a quaint high street. It was full of shoppers. A little crowd had gathered around the lorry, ooh-ing and aah-ing.

'Where'd she go?' she asked desperately. But at the same time she saw Kate walking quickly and stiffly up the high street and, clutching her aching stomach, she set off after her.

The Doctor knew he had only one chance.

The Dalek was unformed, slower and more cautious than a full-grown warrior. It was just as well he'd removed the weapon or by now everyone on the site, including him, would be dead. Without the gun, the Dalek was operating only on its wits, and they weren't quite up to scratch just yet. Even so, his plan – the plan he'd just made up – would take all of his skill to pull off.

He was crouched down inside the cab of the largest crane, right at the far edge of the site. His eyes just peeped over the control board, allowing him a view of a gap between two of the unfinished flats. The Dalek was fixated on him and soon enough it would have to turn that corner. His opportunity to destroy it.

The midday sun glinted off a hint of gold. The Dalek turned the corner.

The Doctor braced himself. He reached up for a lever on the control board with his right hand. His eyes swept keenly across the scene below him, taking everything into account. He waited until the Dalek was exactly between the two walls, with a cliff edge only sixty or so feet behind it.

Then he stood up and gave a loud whistle. 'Over here!' he called.

Just as he'd expected, the Dalek swivelled round, its eye-stalk raised.

The Doctor leaned out of the cab and threw the brick clutched in his left hand. It whizzed through the air and struck the Dalek in the middle of its eye-stalk, its weakest point.

'My vision is impaired!' it shrieked. 'I cannot see!'

The Doctor pulled the lever and the ball attached to the crane – half a ton of lead – smashed into the Dalek's mid-section. The Dalek screeched in surprise and anger as it sailed through the air and then disappeared over the edge of the cliff, spinning as it was lost from view. A second later there was an almighty crash.

The Doctor punched the air and scrambled down from the crane. He ran to the cliff-top and looked down to the sea. The Dalek was lying in the shallow water, the waves lapping over it. Its eye-stalk and sucker moved feebly.

The Doctor took a deep breath and then started to climb down the cliff, moving from handhold to handhold like a monkey. At last he plunged into the water. The Dalek was only a few feet away, croaking and gurgling to itself. He waded towards it, filled with purpose.

It was do or die. And to do, in this case, meant to kill. He had killed millions of Daleks – but never before with his bare hands.

A second later he was using the sonic screwdriver. He ran it along the hinge and ripped open the top section of the Dalek. The mutant inside was now almost complete. Its tentacles were firming up, tightening their grip on the casing's connections. In a few seconds it would be unstoppable; it would use its auto-repair function to repair its eye-stalk and become a truly worthy opponent. He had to act while it was still weak. He had to kill it.

The Doctor hesitated for a second.

'You cannot kill me, Doctor ...' moaned the Dalek. 'You ... will not ... do it.'

'That's an old one. And it doesn't work any longer!'

He adjusted the settings on the sonic screwdriver and plunged it into the casing. It touched the vital life-support connection.

The Doctor gritted his teeth. 'No second chances!' He activated the sonic screwdriver.

The Dalek screamed.

The casing crackled, green sparks flying.

The Doctor was thrown backwards, hurled into the sea. He just had time to notice a fish swimming by before he blacked out.

CHAPTER NINE

KATE WALKED THROUGH THE MARKET, flinching from contact with the humans bustling around her. There were other animals too, flying pests and filthy dogs. The scents of the food products around her were vile. Nutrition was a need, not something to be enjoyed flabbily.

She felt flooded with strength. 'I will be unstoppable!' she shouted out loud.

A few of the humans in the market around her laughed.

'Oh, will you?' said a flat, dull voice behind her.

Kate turned. She knew the voice. It was Serena, shopping bag under her big fat arm.

'Serena,' said Kate, relishing each syllable of the name.

'Do you realise you're sacked?' Serena said, pushing her stupid glasses up her nose. 'I didn't swallow that road accident story for one minute. And now here you are, lunchtime, mooching around the market. Had your hair done, I see. It's been mad this morning. Delays in mattress delivery all over Liverpool and the North-East, people screaming my ears off in Scouse and Geordie. "She'll come in," I kept telling myself. "Even she can't be that irresponsible. Perhaps she was actually telling the truth ..." '

Kate reached out and clamped her hand around Serena's throat. 'Stop your prattling!'

Serena's eyes bulged. Her fleshy, wet mouth struggled for air. One by one, the people in the market who were near enough to see what was happening moved towards Kate. They were screaming for her to let go, but she ignored them and tightened her grip on Serena. She felt gloriously happy.

'I will never have to worry about you again,' she spat, turning Serena from side to side. 'To think, this morning, I was worried about you. Worried what you might say. Worried about my job. Worried about clearing my debts.' She threw back her head and laughed joyfully. 'And you were nothing!'

'Please, Kate ...' Serena pleaded.

'Put her down, Kate!' shouted another voice.

Rose ran up to her, pushing through the astonished crowd.

Kate smirked, shaking Serena like a doll. 'Why?'

'Look, there must be something human left inside you,' Rose told her. 'Your mum and dad, you live with them, don't you?'

'That is not relevant!'

Rose pointed to Serena, who seemed to be on the point of passing out. 'What would your mum say about that? Could you kill that woman and look your mum in the eye?'

The words stirred something in Kate. She imagined her mother's horrified face. A sliver of conscience pricked at her and she relaxed her grip.

Serena dropped to the ground, then got up and stumbled off.

Meanwhile, Kate sank to her knees. 'Rose, please help me.'

The Doctor woke in the water. At first he was only distantly aware of murky shapes and a feeling of floating contentment. Then he remembered.

He shook himself and swam up towards the

light. He burst out of the water, taking in great lungfuls of air. The sonic screwdriver was bobbing in the shallow water a few feet away. He reached out and snatched it up, shook it dry, then looked about, treading water.

He'd been knocked back a fair distance from the cliff edge. He found the landmark of the crane with its wrecking ball on the skyline and looked down.

There was no sign of the Dalek.

He swam over to where it had fallen and cursed under his breath. The casing had repelled him – and stolen electrical energy from the sonic screwdriver. The Dalek was active now, its mind fully formed. Its instinct was to exterminate. What would it do next?

His mouth ran dry. 'Frank,' he said. 'Frank, I'm so sorry.'

He started climbing up the cliff.

Frank couldn't help laughing. He pictured his wife getting in tonight, asking how things had gone at the dig, and him replying that there'd been nothing unusual. He'd just met a doctor who could travel in space and time, and seen the corpse of an alien robot from the planet

Skaro. Oh yeah, and that Doctor, he would be popping in later.

He was on the train back home, his canvas bag on the seat next to him. Despite what he'd said earlier, he did have questions for the Doctor. He wanted the truth – and at the same time he didn't. The Doctor would probably turn out to be just some bloke called Steve with a weird sense of humour.

Frank chuckled again. He found himself almost more willing to believe that the Doctor *was* an alien.

He didn't know why, but there'd been something reassuring about the Doctor. In their brief time together, he'd seemed to represent something timeless. He had given off the comforting sense that no matter how bad the world got, things were going to be OK. Like a parent to a child.

The train ground to a shrieking halt. That was nothing unusual. He heard sighs from the three or four other passengers in the compartment. Frank stared idly out of the window, into someone's back garden, where washing was flying on the line.

Something made a loud clang on top of the

train carriage. This time Frank looked up, startled.

A section of the roof was bulging out, as if an incredibly powerful magnet was pulling at it. The other passengers stood up.

Frank looked towards his canvas bag, his heart pounding.

The roof splintered open, a jagged hole revealing a patch of bright blue sky.

Frank clutched the canvas bag to him. Though he was terrified, a small part of his brain rejoiced. The Doctor *was* for real. There *were* aliens.

Through the gap in the roof the Dalek descended. It gave off power, strength, sinister life. It spoke in a throaty electronic rasp, one syllable at a time, like an old computer in a 1950s B-movie. 'I have detected the weapon in this vehicle. Where is the weapon? Which of you has the weapon?'

One of the other passengers, a girl of about fifteen, screamed and the Dalek zoomed across to her. 'Answer! Answer!'

Frank's hand carefully unbuckled the straps on the bag. Perhaps there was some way he could use the weapon against the Dalek.

The Dalek caught the movement of his hand. 'You will attach the weapon.'

Frank pulled out the gun, his hand shaking, and trained it right at the Dalek. His fingers felt desperately for some kind of trigger, a button or anything ...

'Attach the weapon now! Obey!' screeched the Dalek.

Frank hesitated.

The Dalek's sucker grabbed the girl and flung her down the carriage like a bag of rubbish. 'Obey or the young female dies!'

Frank staggered forward.

'Attach the weapon!' ordered the Dalek. 'Obey!'

Frank remembered the Doctor's description of the Daleks – the most evil things in the universe. He couldn't do it. But then he heard the young girl sobbing at the other end of the carriage. He couldn't not do it.

He walked up and slotted the weapon into its housing. It clicked neatly back in place.

'The Doctor will stop you,' he heard himself say. 'I know him. He'll stop you. He'll save us.'

The Dalek paused before replying, 'The Doctor is not here.'

It raised the gun and Frank closed his eyes.

The Dalek fired and a bolt of energy shot out. Frank screamed, and for a second his body was suspended in the air, his skeleton showing through the dazzling beam of unearthly light.

Then the Dalek turned and picked off the other passengers one by one. It screamed with pleasure and joy, 'Exterminate! Exterminate! Exterminate!'

CHAPTER TEN

POLICE CARS HAD SCREECHED into the pretty market square. Seconds later, Rose found herself surrounded by officers, while the shoppers pointed accusingly at Kate, who was slumped against a lamp-post, sobbing quietly to herself.

'I'm supposed to be looking after her,' she told a policewoman. 'It's all my fault. She needs to get to a hospital far, far away.' She was praying for the Doctor to turn up. Even to her ears, her words sounded feeble.

She watched as the police led Kate to the car. There was nothing she could do.

Suddenly there were screams. The sound of crashing cars. Running feet. A distant metallic voice cried, 'Exterminate!'

The police and shoppers turned their heads towards these weird sounds.

Rose felt her stomach flip over. 'Oh, no. No, you're kidding me ...'

*

It was now twenty past twelve. People were starting to come out of the building societies, shoe shops, baker's shops and butcher's shops along Twyford high street, crowding on to the narrow pavements.

A column of smoke was rising from the far side of town.

The Dalek appeared through it, its gun arm waving in all directions, strafing the street with sizzling bolts of deadly radiation.

A middle-aged woman got out of her car to run for cover. The Dalek fired again. Her skeleton glowed green as she was cut down without mercy.

The Dalek saw humans crowded in a window. It fired. The glass shattered and the humans backed away, running into their offices, screaming. The Dalek zoomed over, turned its midsection, thrust its gun through the smashed window frame and blasted them one after another.

Then it sped down the high street, chasing the fleeing, panicking humans.

'Where is the other?' it called. 'Where is the one called Kate?'

*

Crouched behind a bin in the now deserted market square, Rose and Kate heard the voice. Kate instantly leapt to her feet.

'No!' shouted Rose, grabbing her, trying to hold her back.

When she looked into Kate's eyes, she knew the battle for her mind was lost. The tears dried and the life went out of them. Her face took on an expression of twisted pride.

Kate flicked Rose away. 'There is nothing you can do now,' she said. 'The Dalek factor is too powerful.'

Rose got up and pointed towards the high street, towards the smoke and ringing alarms. There were bodies all over the ground.

'Look at that! Think of your mum, your dad!'

'Family connections are a genetic weakness,' Kate said in a flat voice. 'They are weak and unnecessary.' She stalked away.

The Dalek appeared through the smoke. It was now shining and gleaming. The casing could have been brand new. Rose guessed it had taken electrical energy from somewhere to repair itself.

Kate and the Dalek moved towards each

other. Kate bowed her head.

'Master, what are my orders?'

The Dalek pointed to Rose. 'The other humans have fled. Who is this one?'

'Rose. A companion of the Doctor.'

'Yeah,' shouted Rose proudly. 'You know, the Doctor, the man you're so afraid of.'

The Dalek swung its gun to cover her. 'I am not afraid,' it said as if it were deeply offended. 'Daleks do not fear. Must not fear.' It moved closer and the blue glow in its eye seemed to stare right through her. 'You have an emotional connection to the Doctor.'

Rose swallowed and stepped back.

'The Doctor will be weakened by your death,' the Dalek continued. 'It is a Dalek directive to weaken the Doctor.' The gun swivelled in its socket.

Rose closed her eyes.

Then she heard the distant roar of ancient, alien engines.

She opened her eyes to see the side of the TARDIS standing right in front of her. She heard the Dalek fire. The bolt bounced off the battered wooden doors. Then the Doctor emerged. He looked wet and scruffy but he was smiling in an angry, dangerous way. He turned to face the Dalek.

'I see you've got your gun back,' he said quietly. 'Easy to find you. Not many people firing high-energy lasers around here today.' Something in his voice was different, more emotional than usual. He raised his hands.

'Come on, then, exterminate!'

CHAPTER ELEVEN

ROSE HURRIED TO the Doctor's side. He waved his hands in front of the Dalek. 'Come on. Fire. Even you can't miss at this range.' He nodded to Kate. 'Oh, and you've got a girlfriend now, have you? About time. We were all starting to wonder.'

The Dalek lowered its gun.

'It won't kill you,' said Rose. 'So it wants something from you?'

'Of course it does,' said the Doctor. 'It needs knowledge. That old data store it's using is out of date. It wants to take the knowledge from my mind. Am I right?'

'That knowledge is of value,' said the Dalek.

'We can discuss having my brain sucked out later, over a burger perhaps,' said the Doctor, rubbing his hands together. 'But first I want a few explanations.' He strolled over to the Dalek casually.

'Stay back!' shouted the Dalek.

'Yeah, not afraid at all,' called Rose.

'Come on, then. Let's get the whole story. Because after I've destroyed you, Rose over there's gonna be full of questions. You know, yatter-yatter in my ear, how did it come to life in the first place and all that. So you might as well tell her now.'

Rose could see that beneath his jokiness the Doctor was actually furious.

The Dalek faced the Doctor squarely. In an even louder voice than usual, it began. 'My glorious Dalek ancestors –'

'Oh, here we go,' sighed the Doctor. 'Couldn't resist showing off, could you?' He smiled at Rose. 'I can play a Dalek like an old fiddle.'

'My glorious Dalek ancestors,' the Dalek repeated, 'sent a time capsule back to Earth. It arrived here centuries ago. Its mission was to spread the Dalek factor to all humans and use their life force to create back-up from raw matter.'

'How embarrassing for you,' said the Doctor. 'The mighty race of Daleks, so weakened they needed help from the humans they despise. A last, desperate gamble. To alter the genetics of the human race. And judging from that scented candle shop over there, it didn't work.'

The Dalek continued, 'The capsule was blasted towards Earth in the final battle of the Time War. Its engines failed on the journey. My ancestor, the owner of this casing, ejected and fell to Earth.'

'Where it let go a little bit of Dalek factor, just a whiff,' said the Doctor, 'before it died. It caught on to some humans. Not active, but always there in their genes, handed down from generation to generation. Probably only one in half a billion have got it now, including Kate over there.'

'The Dalek factor was triggered when this casing was disturbed by the humans digging,' continued the Dalek. 'Kate answered the call. Her Dalek life force was used to bring to life a new Dalek from the data stored in the casing.'

'Nifty,' said the Doctor. He raised his voice. 'But this is where it stops.' He suddenly became more serious. 'You have two options: destroy yourself or I will destroy you. Up to you.'

'You cannot destroy me!' shrieked the Dalek.

The Doctor leaned up close and whispered simply, 'Wanna bet?'

'There is another option, Doctor,' it replied.

'A choice for you to make.'

The Doctor blinked. Rose could tell he hadn't been expecting this.

'I offer you a deal,' said the Dalek.

The Doctor laughed. 'In the old days I knew a few people who did deals with Daleks. What happened to them? Let's see if I remember. Oh yeah, they all ended up being exterminated. In the back, usually.'

The Dalek ignored him. 'I know of your emotional attachment to this planet. I can kill all the humans. But I am prepared to spare Earth and its people.'

The Doctor bit his lip. 'For what?'

'You must give me the power to escape. The means to travel in space and time. I wish to travel to another planet. I will give you the space-time coordinates for my journey.'

'And what'll you do there, settle down to a quiet retirement? Or, I dunno, build a new race of Daleks perhaps?'

'The Daleks will be reborn,' said the Dalek. 'But I will spare Earth. I will spare the woman Rose and all the other humans.'

'And some other planet, they all get killed,'

said Rose.

'There is no choice. In a crisis, impure creatures care only for the ones they know. This is a weakness.' The Dalek was speaking to the Doctor. 'The Doctor will not allow me to destroy your planet. To kill your family.'

The Doctor turned pale. He looked over at Rose. 'It's right. It can play me like an old fiddle.'

'You're gonna give it what it wants?'

The Doctor nodded. 'Nothing else I can do. I can't let Earth be destroyed.'

'But this other planet and all the others out there ...'

'They will be exterminated!' the Dalek exulted. 'And the new race of Daleks will be born. Daleks of my creation!'

CHAPTER TWELVE

THE DOCTOR WALKED SLOWLY into the TARDIS. It was clear that he wasn't happy. Rose followed, slamming the door quickly after her.

'How convincing was I?' she said. 'I deserve an Oscar for that.'

The Doctor looked at her grimly. 'I wasn't bluffing.'

'I know you. You're gonna fix up some booby trap, send the Dalek flying off into the space-time vortex or something, kill it.'

The Doctor shook his head and said gently, 'Rose, that Dalek is a genius. An expert in space-time engineering. If I try any kind of trick, it'll see it a mile off.'

Rose watched as he strode over to a shadowy corner of the TARDIS and pulled out a huge, old-fashioned trunk. 'But you can't actually do it!'

'I can save Earth,' said the Doctor. He swung open the lid of the trunk. 'For a Dalek, that's a good deal.'

'People who do deals with Daleks ...' Rose reminded him.

'Even if I was the sort of person who liked pulling triggers, do you know anything that could stop that Dalek? It's fully formed now. I can't just throw a brick at it again. It's got a tough, radiation-proof casing. It's immune to every infection. It'd just blink at a nuclear explosion. If it could blink.' He rooted through the trunk, which contained a weird collection of jumble.

Rose came up close to him. 'We destroyed them before,' she said seriously. 'I destroyed them.' She remembered becoming the bad wolf, looking into the time vortex, wiping away a million Daleks with the wave of one hand.

'Try that again and you could take the whole universe down with you,' said the Doctor. 'This is the only way. Here.' He'd found what he was looking for in the trunk and held it up for her to see. It was a thick metal bangle decorated with a strange seal. 'It's old, but I reckon I can get it going.' He buzzed the sonic screwdriver over the seal and it glowed gently. 'Time Ring, it's like a personal TARDIS. Could take you anywhere.'

Rose stared at him. 'So we're really selling out? Letting it go?'

The Doctor looked down sadly. Then he gently stroked her cheek. 'Either option is a nightmare. But the Dalek was right.' He gazed over her shoulder, looking into the past. 'We go back a long, long time. The Dalek knows me. It knows I can't stand back and watch it destroy your home.'

Kate the human Dalek watched the Doctor and Rose emerge from the TARDIS. She was filled with devotion and righteous anger. It was time for her master to leave this pathetic planet and secure the true destiny of the Daleks.

'One Time Ring,' said the Doctor, twirling it casually round his finger. 'So, where do you want to go?'

The Dalek scanned the bangle. 'The device is acceptable. Attach it.'

The Doctor slipped the bangle over the sucker arm.

'I cannot operate the control panel,' said the Dalek. 'It is designed for human operation. The one called Kate will set the coordinates.'

Kate stepped forward eagerly. Her fingers

91

touched the seal of the bangle and instantly her Dalek brain recognised its design and its workings.

'I am ready,' she said.

'Seven zero five nine galactic north by eight eight point five galactic west,' said the Dalek. 'Time factor: Earth date AD 500 million.'

Kate's fingers danced over the seal, setting the coordinates.

'Very smart,' the Doctor said, nodding. 'The most peaceful time in future history,' he added for Rose's benefit.

The Dalek lowered its eye-stalk. 'The impure creatures of this future time care about peace. They know nothing of war, nothing of the Daleks. The one called Kate will come with me. She will plead for materials to rebuild my race. The creatures will supply them without asking questions. When we are ready, we shall emerge to conquer and destroy!'

Rose took the Doctor's arm. 'No,' she said firmly. 'It sounds far away. It gets us off the hook, but those people in the future are just like us. We can't do it!'

The bangle began to pulsate with golden light. 'Stand back,' barked the Dalek.

The Doctor and Rose obeyed.

The Dalek fixed its eye in the Doctor. 'You will not follow.'

'Never crossed my mind,' said the Doctor innocently.

'You will not follow. Because you will no longer exist.' The Dalek raised its gun, aiming right at the Doctor. 'The last thing I see before I depart will be your extermination!'

'Of course,' said the Doctor simply. 'I made a deal with a Dalek. What do you think I expected? A handshake and a box of Terry's All Gold?'

'Activate the Time Ring!' screeched the Dalek.

Kate's fingers moved over the controls.

She heard Rose's voice. 'Kate, please. What's inside you – fight it. I know you can!'

'You waste energy,' said Kate. 'The Dalek factor is too strong.'

Rose ran to Kate's side. 'Listen. All that stuff in your head. All the millions of planets and billions of years. I know what it's like. Forget it. This morning, you missed the bus. What was the number of that bus?'

'That is not important,' said Kate. But she saw the bus, the silly rural single-decker, turning the corner on to the green. The number was 354.

Rose carried on desperately. 'Toby, your ex, the one who spent all the credit on your card. What did he look like?' Kate saw Toby, thinning hair and paunch, the kind of man you settle for when there's nothing else going. 'What did you have for tea last night?' Rose cried. 'Custard?' It was the first word that came into her head.

Custard. Gloopy, yellow, pointless, tasty custard. Kate had never thought about custard before. Not thought hard about it. The Dalek part of her dismissed it. The human part imagined it pouring thickly over bread and butter pudding. She realised she hadn't eaten for hours.

But it was too late. The Dalek fired. 'Exterminate the Doctor!'

A glowing sphere of light formed around the Dalek. The blast fizzed harmlessly inside it.

The Doctor clapped his hands together. 'Custard!' he cried. 'She's put a force field around the Dalek! Humans get hungry. What else do they do? Small things, big things, anything! We can reach her, get her to destroy it! Rose!'

Rose took his cue. *'The X Factor,'* she gabbled. 'Floor polish. Contact lenses. Waiting for home delivery, some time between eight and six. Gas bills.' She tried desperately to think. 'People talking too loud on their phones in trains. Pointless internet arguments, with people you don't even know. Kylie. When they ask "Do you have a Boots advantage card?"'

The Doctor took over, speaking quickly and passionately. 'Then there are the best human qualities. They're inside you, Kate, and I've seen them. The potential that is bursting from every human. The explorer, determined to see something nobody's seen before. Writing home to tell his wife he's never coming back, he knows he's gonna die, but he must tell her he loves her.' He gestured to Rose. 'More!'

'My mum,' she said, 'waiting up for me in her dressing gown till gone three, then pretending she just got up to put the kettle on.' She grabbed another example from her own life. 'When your mates are talking, and you close your eyes and it's the most beautiful sound in the world, just people you love talking rubbish!'

'Heroes!' snapped the Doctor, as he stepped forward, eyes alight. 'Running into a fire to save someone else's child. People struggling, surviving, together. There was a time, thousands of years back, when there were only a few hundred humans left – I saw them – I saw them say no, we will go on, and they made it, and filled the world!' He gasped for breath. 'It's the whole messy, glorious human thing!'

'The Dalek factor will triumph!' shrieked the Dalek. It fired again and again, the beams dissolving into the sphere of light.

Kate's mind was divided. Down the middle.

On the Dalek side there was power, glory, calm. Cities made of steel and oceans of ooze, stretching away into infinity under red moonlight. There was anger, purpose, absolute devotion.

On the human side there was muddle. Daftness, regrets, accidents. Headaches and lost tickets and scratched CDs out of their cases and missed appointments and embarrassment. Apologies and blown chances. Being ill. Christmas. Half-hearted sex. Wogan and his nonsense.

But there was more to that muddle. There were beautiful buildings, all different, jammed together any old way under nights full of diamond stars. There was the thrill of making a new friend. There was music that never stopped changing. There were new ideas, new jokes, new discoveries, pouring out of that human chaos.

And Mum and Dad, taking her back in, giving her chance after chance after chance.

For one second Kate rejected the Dalek factor. In that vital second her fingers, with all their Dalek knowledge intact but with human resolve, flickered across the control unit of the Time Ring.

And instead of disappearing, the Dalek started to vibrate. A thick buzzing hum filled the air.

'I dunno what I just did ...' Kate told the Doctor and Rose.

'Never mind now. Come on!' shouted the Doctor.

Kate suddenly felt very confused, as if this strange day was finally catching up with her. Then something clicked in her head. 'Self-destruct. I've set the Time Ring thing to self-destruct.'

'Yes!' cried the Doctor. 'And on the other hand, no! Warp implosion!' He grabbed Kate and Rose, pulling them towards the TARDIS. 'Run!'

He couldn't resist one last look back at the Dalek.

'You cannot escape!' it ranted. 'Exterminate – exterminate –' It was rattling uncontrollably now, becoming a wobbling golden blur.

'You got it wrong,' the Doctor sneered. 'Your great plan failed. It was a balls-up. And you know why? Because who wants to be a Dalek, when they could be a human?' He waved jauntily and said, 'Goodbye,' with quiet, satisfied contempt.

Then he ran into the TARDIS after Kate and Rose.

The door slammed shut. The TARDIS faded away, ancient engines groaning.

The Dalek gave one last roar of anger before it imploded, its atoms blasted into nothingness. There was a mighty boom and every single window in a twenty-mile radius blew out.

Then there was only silence, and a smoking black patch in the quiet market town where the last Dalek had stood only moments before.

CHAPTER THIRTEEN

'THAT WAS BRILLIANT!' cried the Doctor. 'Come here!' He picked Kate up and whirled her round the TARDIS.

'Stop it! Please put me down,' said Kate a little crossly.

The Doctor obeyed with a joyful bow, as if he was finishing a dance.

Kate looked round at the weird, gloomy room. 'Where is this? There was just a box ...'

Rose was intrigued. Kate seemed to have forgotten everything. As a Dalek, she'd known all about the Doctor and the TARDIS. 'She's lost it?'

The Doctor nodded. 'No Dalek, no Dalek factor. Just a lot of harmless, useless genes going back to sleep.'

Kate touched her head. 'What about my hair?'

Rose handed her a mirror from the jumble in the trunk. 'Red.'

Kate sighed. 'No offence, but that's how I prefer it.' She yawned. She was exhausted.

But the Doctor wasn't going to let her rest. 'You are a hero! Hero! Hero!' he said.

'OK, Doctor,' said Rose. 'Leave her alone.'

'She's just prevented a disaster for the universe! She played a blinder!' He turned back to Kate. 'What can I do for you?'

'I'd really like to go home,' said Kate in a small voice.

'Yeah, that's easy, we're doing that. There must be something else, though,' said the Doctor. 'Come on. You're not gonna get the chance again.'

Rose stepped forward. 'Got your credit card on you?'

Kate handed it over to Rose, who gave it to the Doctor. 'You could pay off this.'

The Doctor took the card happily and ran the sonic screwdriver along the magnetic strip on the back. 'All gone. But I've battered your credit rating for ever. Don't even try applying for another one. No second chances.' He tossed the card into the trunk.

Another thought struck Kate. 'Oh, my God. I grabbed my boss. Tried to strangle her. In front of everyone in Twyford.'

'No problem,' said the Doctor confidently.

'It is a problem,' said Rose.

'No problem,' the Doctor insisted. 'What colour hair did this madwoman have? Natural blonde. That's not you, is it? Just looked like you.'

Kate stared at the two of them. The Dalek factor was gone, but she still had a sense of what their lives must be like. 'Today. That was like a normal day for you, yeah?'

Rose grinned. 'Just about.'

'Then the two of you are mad, aren't you?' said Kate.

The TARDIS door opened on to the village green. Kate stepped out and set off towards her parents' house. She didn't look back as the blue box faded away.

Her head was full of plans. For the first time in years she had no debt. She'd ring her mate Lucy in London tonight. She could get out of Winchelham, start over again in the city. She could stay over at Lucy's for a couple of weeks. Lucy wouldn't mind, not really. Then she'd get a job up there. She would get a bloke, a proper bloke this time. Perhaps she could even get the flip-flop business going again.

She walked back into the world of compromise, making do, muddling along, bread and butter pudding with custard, and heroes. The world that she had saved.

CHAPTER FOURTEEN

THE SUN BLAZED DOWN on Durham University in the summer of 1970.

Frank Openshaw crossed the courtyard on the way to his next history lecture. He brushed the long hair out of his eyes and lifted his new canvas bag, from the army surplus shop, more comfortably on to his shoulder.

A third-year was walking towards him. She was gorgeous, but he didn't stand a chance with someone like her, so he put it out of his mind.

Suddenly a blonde teenage girl, wearing a weird hooded top, crashed into him on a bicycle. It seemed almost deliberate. The third-year hurried over, helped them both up.

'Sorry,' said the blonde girl.

'Try looking where you're going,' said the third-year, sharing an amused glance with Frank. Her eyes lingered on him a second too long.

The blonde girl got back on to her bike and cycled off.

GARETH ROBERTS

'Are you OK?' asked the third-year, putting a concerned hand on Frank's shoulder. 'I'm Sandra, by the way.'

He shook her hand. 'Frank.'

Rose wheeled the bike to a stop outside the TARDIS, which was parked in the arch leading off the courtyard. Through the arch the Doctor watched Frank and Sandra walking away together.

'That what you wanted?' asked Rose, climbing off the bike.

'Yes,' said the Doctor. He took Rose's hand.

'What was it for anyway?'

The Doctor opened the door of the TARDIS. 'Bending the rules. For my friend.'

Acknowledgements

Thanks to Helen Raynor, Justin Richards and Stuart Cooper. And to Clayton Hickman, Neil Corry and the Not Players.

WORLD BOOK DAY

Quick Reads

Quick Reads are published alongside and in partnership with BBC RaW.

We would like to thank all our partners in the *Quick* Reads project for all their help and support:

Department for Education and Skills
Trades Union Congress
The Vital Link
The Reading Agency
National Literacy Trust

Quick Reads would also like to thank the Arts Council England and National Book Tokens for their sponsorship.

We would also like to thank the following companies for providing their services free of charge: SX Composing for typesetting all the titles; Icon Reproduction for text reproduction; Norske Skog, Stora Enso, PMS and Iggusend for paper/board supplies; Mackays of Chatham, Cox and Wyman, Bookmarque, White Quill Press, Concise, Norhaven and GGP for the printing.

www.worldbookday.com